The Saving of
Okee and Dokee
Sea Turtle

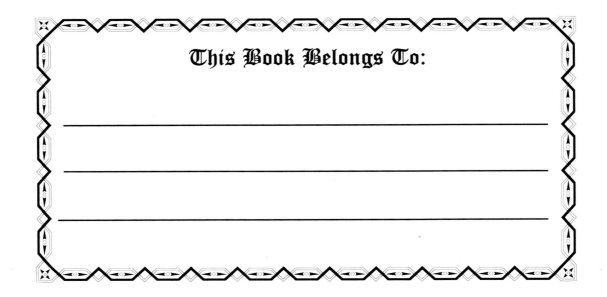

This Book Belongs To:

The Saving of Okee and Dokee Sea Turtle

by John Harms II

Illustrated by Robin Lee Makowski

Edited by Denise H. Belizar

Frederick Press ~ Palm Beach Gardens, Florida USA

Library of Congress Catalog Card Number 00-133061

ISBN 0-9653871-4-3

Printed in China

Dedicated to my sister Terri, a true lover of books,

for her encouragement during our school years.

Special thanks to:

Susan D. Schenk of The Marinelife Center of Juno Beach, Florida USA

Company Philosophy

Frederick Press strives to inspire children to realize the importance of caring for their local environment through a positive, active role. By learning about interesting animals that are common to certain areas, children can better understand the needs of their own surroundings. Frederick Press hopes children will become more aware of their natural environment, by enjoying the adventures of a boy named Buster and the animals he encounters.

When people take proper care of their local environment and are responsible when visiting other areas, the earth's ecology will improve and the world will be a better place for all living things.

Frederick Press donates a portion of its revenue to benefit the rehabilitation of injured and orphaned animals, support zoological parks, and save manatees.

TABLE OF CONTENTS

*Glossary words are *italicized* throughout the story for easy reference.

CHAPTER 1

~ *Turtle Watching* ~

Buster couldn't wait. The beauty of the moon illuminating the *sea grapes* and gumbo limbo trees filled him with excitement. He jumped out of the car onto the soft sandy path that led to the beach.

"Buster! Don't go running off now. Jake Fisher and Rob will be here any minute," his dad ordered.

"It's just so awesome out here with the full moon. Can you hear the owl, Dad?" Buster replied as he jogged back to the car.

Buster's whole family was there, even Claire, his big sister.

A pair of headlights turned down the path toward them. Buster could barely make out Jake's dusty old white pickup truck through the glare.

"They're here Dad! Let's get to the beach."

"Just hold on, son. We don't want to scare any turtles from the beach."

Being a wildlife officer, Mr. Fisher was very concerned about nesting sea turtles. Stepping out of the truck, he reached behind his seat for his note pad and flashlight to record his findings. Rob grabbed a light from the back of the pickup and flashed it on Buster. Buster dodged the light to stay in the dark.

"Let's not get carried away, Rob," warned Mr. Fisher. "The turtles are skittish and we don't want them to avoid the beach. Use the flashlight sparingly."

"Hi, Jack! Is everybody ready?" Mr. Fisher said to Buster's dad in his southern drawl.

Walking down the moonlit path, they made their way through the thick overgrowth. The subtropical forest sounds sang in Buster's ears. The cicada buzzed. The tiny *narrow-mouth frogs* sounded like sheep braying. Every once in a while an owl would hoot. The shadows on the ground seemed to dance with the animal music.

Reaching the first ridge overlooking the beach, they all looked down and watched in shock. A sea turtle was swimming only a few yards from shore, when a bright light flashed in her eyes. Immediately she dove under the water and swam to the safety of deep water.

On the beach, a group of people yelled to each other, breaking the tranquility. "Did you see that turtle! Get your cameras ready, and remember your flash."

The sea turtle surfaced from beyond the reach of the lights and waited. She only had a few days left to lay her eggs so they would hatch safely. Her homing instincts were strong; she wouldn't lay her eggs on any other beach. This was where she had hatched.

The people became impatient and wandered off without seeing the turtle again. Mr. Fisher and Buster's family reached the shore to find it deserted.

"I hope they didn't scare the turtles away for the night," Rob said as he reached the beach.

Mr. Fisher, Rob and Buster scouted the area for signs of turtle activity. They found fresh track indentations along with flipper marks in the sand. Following the tracks up from the ocean, they discovered a new nest.

Mr. Fisher made an entry in his *logbook* to record the nest's location. Buster's dad took a wooden stake marked with the log information and put it by the spot so the nest could be monitored.

"Let's see if that turtle returns tonight to nest," Mr. Fisher said softly as he turned off his flashlight. "Be very still and quiet; speak only in whispers."

Claire spread a blanket on the beach so everyone could relax as they waited patiently.

CHAPTER 2

~ Gerty's Return ~

An hour later, the turtle returned to shore. It set its flipper on dry ground for the first time in a few years. Buster could see the silhouette in the moonlight as it slowly crawled up the beach. She would stop for a moment and scan the area for signs of danger.

Buster held his breath. The turtle looked right at him. He felt his heart skip. "Would she go back to the water?" Buster worried.

Finally, she continued. Buster breathed a sigh of relief.

No one said a word as the turtle slowly started to dig her nest. Even Buster's younger brother was quiet, awestruck by the scene; he grabbed hold of his mother's hand.

The turtle used her flippers like shovels, lifting the sand away until the hole was about two feet deep. Then she began laying her eggs. After she settled in to lay her batch of over one hundred eggs, it was safe for Mr. Fisher to turn on his flashlight. The turtle was covered with barnicles and algae.

"She's been tagged," Mr. Fisher said softly as he recorded the number, "and she appears to be in excellent health."

"Dad! What about her flipper?" Rob asked, as he looked with concern at her right fore flipper. The flipper was only half as long as the left side.

"That happened when she was very small," Mr. Fisher explained. "She got tangled in some discarded fishing line and lost part of her flipper. The rehab center put a tag on her for identification, and kept her until she recovered. They named her Gerty."

"Why is she crying?" Claire asked.

"My father told me a tale about turtles when I was a little boy," Mr. Fisher whispered.

"He said, 'She is crying because she is both happy and sad. She is happy because she will have children from her eggs. She is sad because she will never see her young.'"

Buster's dad added, "Today people say she tears because it eliminates salt from her body."

Claire liked the old tale better.

When she was through laying her eggs, the turtle began covering her nest with her flippers. She gave out what seemed to Buster's mom to be a sigh of relief, then headed back to the water. Mr. Fisher placed another stake in the sand and marked the nest on the map.

"We need to watch this one; it's very close to the storm line. We may have to move it if a *tropical storm* threatens the area."

On the way back from the beach, no one spoke a word. They were all thinking about the mother turtle and all the eggs she had laid.

The next day Mr. Fisher, Rob and Buster stopped at the beach house headquarters for the turtle census, and Mr. Fisher added his report to the master map. Rob and Buster waited in the living room, looking at some of the interesting exhibits collected on turtle watches. Some things, like the turtle shells, were donated by families that had settled in the area before the county was founded.

"Wow! What a beautiful shell," Buster exclaimed as he ran his fingers over the smooth surface. "The turtle we saw last night had barnacles and moss all over it. I didn't know they were so pretty."

"That's a hawksbill turtle," a voice said behind him. "It's endangered now because of man's *exploitation*."

Buster turned to see Mrs. Halihan, head of the Turtle Center, coming down the stairs.

"Mrs. Halihan, what's this big turtle shell? It's taller than dad," Rob asked wide-eyed, pointing to the large shell in the corner.

"That's a leatherback. They're rare in our area," she replied.

"Marian, good to see you today. You remember my son Rob, and this is his friend, Buster," Mr. Fisher said as he entered the room from the office.

"My, it's nice to meet such interested children," said Mrs. Halihan. "Would you like something to drink, boys?"

"We're fine, Mrs. Halihan, thank you," Rob and Buster answered politely.

"Is the weather radio still working?" Mr. Fisher asked. "There's news about a *tropical depression* in the Caicos Islands."

"I must tell you, Jake, they said it has turned into *Tropical Storm* Henry. It may be heading our way," Mrs. Halihan said in a very serious tone.

"We'd better keep an eye on it. Some of the nests won't make it through a full-fledged hurricane," Mr. Fisher added.

"Dad, why don't we move the nests now?" Rob questioned.

"Turtle eggs are easily damaged when they're disturbed. So if we move them without cause we may do more damage than good," Mr. Fisher reasoned. "We'll stop by the hardware store on the way home and pick up a hurricane map, so we can see what's happening with the storm."

Over the next few days, the boys kept very close track of *Tropical Storm* Henry by listening to Buster's AM radio. They plotted and recorded each new position and wind speed, and projected the storm's path. To their relief, the storm looked as if it would pass to the east of Florida and parallel the coast.

"Dad, it looks like the storm will miss us," Rob mentioned with a sigh of relief.

"Yes, we'll be OK, but the waves it produces could still destroy the nests. We need to watch Henry even closer now that it will be due east of us," Mr. Fisher answered in a concerned voice.

CHAPTER 3

~ *Rescue, Rehabilitation, and Release* ~

Several days later, high seas began to threaten Gerty's nest. Mr. Fisher took Rob and Buster to the nest site. The beach was showing signs of bad erosion. The waves were relentless. Each set came in like a hungry monster cutting away at the beach.

"We'd better move Gert's nest before the waves reach it," Mr. Fisher said, as he kneeled down and started digging with his hands.

When they reached the eggs, Mr. Fisher carefully dotted the tops with a safe marker to keep them in the right position, then lifted them out of the nest. He quickly moved above the storm line where the waves wouldn't reach, and dug a hole to match the one Gerty had dug. When the hole was the right depth, the eggs were placed carefully inside it. After the last egg was in place, Mr. Fisher and the boys covered them with sand. Mr. Fisher changed the nest's marker position on the map.

Finishing their task, Buster and Rob searched for the unbroken shells the waves were uncovering. They laughed as they dodged the waves, getting soaked and covered with sand. All of a sudden, a wave cut through the sand and opened up a nest that no one had recorded.

"Dad! Dad! The waves broke open a nest," Rob screamed.

Mr. Fisher ran over to the nest, marked the tops of the eggs, and placed as many of them as he could in Buster and Rob's outstretched t-shirts. They cradled the eggs as gently as possible to keep them from rolling.

The nest was gone almost as soon as the wave opened it. Of the hundred plus eggs in the nest, Buster had twelve in his shirt; Rob had eight.

Mr. Fisher helped the children over the ridge that the waves had made and looked at the eggs.

"Well, you have twenty all together. We'll try to rebury them, but they've been bounced around a lot. I don't think there's much hope for them," he lamented.

"Dad, can we bury them in an area where we can watch over them?" Rob asked, putting them down gently in a bucket.

"There's a fenced maintenance yard by the beach the town uses for erosion control. I'll call Richard at the maintenance shack on the radio," Mr. Fisher answered as they reached the truck.

"Jake Fisher to Maintenance Number One, come in Maintenance One."

"Maintenance One here. Hello, Jake."

"Hi, Richard. We just found an unmarked turtle nest that's been washed out. Can we use your beach maintenance yard as a nest site?" Jake asked.

"Sure. We'll just have to move some things, and then put a sign around the nest," Richard answered.

The boys jumped into the truck and cradled the bucket with the eggs. Mr. Fisher drove to the maintenance yard and met Richard by the gate.

Motioning to them he said, "Come on in. I've got an area cleared, and I've even dug a hole for the eggs."

The nest site was about 75 feet from the waves. The boys gently placed the eggs in the bottom and carefully covered them, just as they'd seen Mr. Fisher do. Fencing was placed over

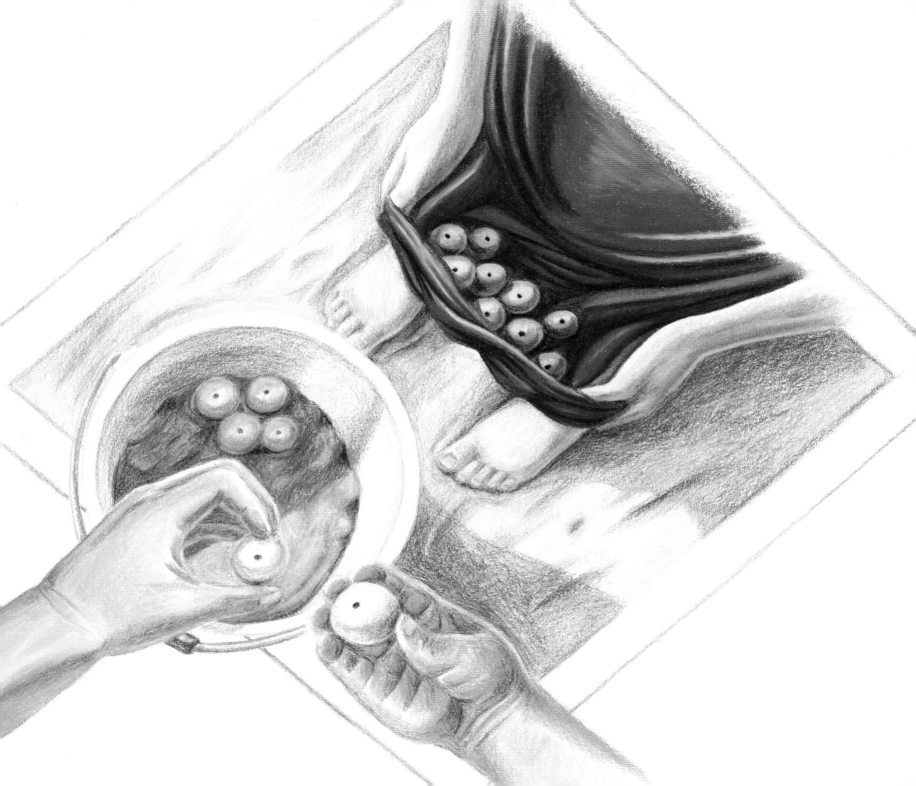

the nest to protect it from *predators*.

"In about 60 days, they should hatch. Then we'll see how many of them survived. You boys did a terrific job. I'm sure some will live," Mr. Fisher said, patting Rob's head and roughing up Buster's hair.

As the time approached, Mr. Fisher found Gerty's nest had hatched. Meanwhile, Buster and Rob researched the best way to help the *hatchlings* survive. They also turned to Mrs. Halihan for help.

"Mrs. Halihan, we found out that only about one in a thousand sea turtles survives to maturity. Is there some way we can help them?" they asked.

Mrs. Halihan answered, "When baby sea turtles hatch, they run for the water. Everything from fire ants and ghost crabs to birds and animals are after them. If they make it to the water, they swim out to the weed line to hide from *predators*. We'll pick up the *hatchlings* and have one of the local boat captains take them out to the weed line."

The maintenance department kept watch on the nest daily; finally, just as Richard was closing one night, he saw movement in the sand. He immediately called Mr. Fisher.

"It looks like they're coming out tonight. Come over right away if you don't want to miss them," Richard warned.

Jake, Rob, Buster, his family and Richard gathered around the area in the maintenance yard by the beach and waited. It was like a group of expectant fathers waiting for their young to be born. Suddenly, the sand moved. A small head popped out, then flippers and a shell. Baby turtle number one started to scamper for the ocean. Then another, and another. Buster counted ten.

As the hatchling turtles scurried on the beach, Buster and Rob picked them up and placed them gently in a bucket with moist sand in the bottom.

After the nest site was quiet for some time, Mr. Fisher uncovered the nest to find the other ten eggs. Eight never developed, but there were two trapped below the undeveloped eggs. Lifting the turtles, Mr. Fisher carefully held them in the palm of his hand. The turtles hardly moved as Mr. Fisher gave them to Buster's dad to place in a special bucket.

"These two are very exhausted from trying to dig through the others. We'll have to look after them until they're strong enough to make it on their own," said Mr. Fisher.

The Turtle Center stayed open late to get the ten turtles ready for their early boat ride in the morning. Buster, Rob and their dads each picked up the turtles and placed them in the tank. Immediately the turtles swam to the seaweed and hid. Even Claire held one, while Marian measured it.

The two straggler turtles were put in a special shallow tank so they could touch bottom while being able to breath.

"Before we release them, we'll make sure they are healthy enough to survive. You boys can help if you'd like," Mrs. Halihan said, smiling.

"Can we, Dad? Can we?" The boys said in unison.

"I don't see any reason why you couldn't," Buster's dad said as he hugged Buster.

"You boys have done an excellent job," Mr. Fisher said, rubbing Rob's head. "It's your project. By the way, what are you going to call them?"

"I'm going to call mine Okee, the Seminole word for water," Rob informed his dad.

"Well, if you're going to call yours Okee, I'm calling mine Dokee," Buster declared.

As the days passed, Okee and Dokee became increasingly active. The time had come to release them at the weed line in the ocean. Mrs. Halihan arranged for Buster, Rob and their dads to accompany the turtles on the boat. Okee and Dokee were placed in a separate bucket for the trip, so Buster and Rob could recognize them from the other turtles being released.

At the dock, three manatees swam by as they boarded the boat. Buster knew it was Sly and his family, from the scars on Sly's mother's back. Sly rolled once, and the family disappeared.

Buster and Rob smiled at each other, remembering when they helped Sly.

The seas were calm as the fishing boat headed out to sea. Buster watched the sun rise on the horizon. A few clouds turned golden as the darkness fell away.

When they reached the weed line, Buster and Rob stood by the bucket that Okee and Dokee were in and gently lifted them out. The turtles were so active, they had a difficult time just holding them. They said goodbye to their turtles, and then lowered them down into the water. Watching Okee and Dokee swim until they disappeared in the shadows of the seaweed, Rob and Buster looked at each other with a sense of accomplishment. They knew that with the help of everyone, the sea turtles would be okey-dokey.

After releasing a few other turtles that had recuperated, the boat headed towards shore.

"What's your next adventure going to be?" Buster's dad asked, smiling, as they watched the weed line fade into the distance.

"I don't know," Buster said, smiling back at his dad. "But it'll be exciting!"

The End

Glossary

Exploitation: To take advantage of something for selfish reasons.

Hatchling: A young reptile, bird or fish recently emerged from an egg.

Logbook: A notebook that is used to record valuable information. Mr. Fisher's logbook kept track of where and when a turtle made its nest, and also, if known, the health of the turtle that laid the eggs.

Narrow-mouth Frogs: A small frog from 7/8" to 1-1/2" found in the southeastern United States along ponds and ditches. Its call is similar to the bleating noise of a sheep.

Predator: An animal that hunts and eats other animals.

Sea Grape: A small tree with large round leaves with clusters of edible fruit that grow like grapes. It can survive near saltwater sources.

Tropical Depression: An ocean storm with winds that revolve counter-clockwise around a center of low pressure, with winds less than 39 miles per hour.

Tropical Storm: A storm with a counter-clockwise wind rotation having wind speeds above 39 miles per hour. Tropical storms develop from tropical depressions. Tropical storms are given names so their movements are easier for people to track.

More About Sea Turtles

Loggerhead turtles are among the most common sea turtles in the world, yet they are considered threatened. All other sea turtles are endangered.

Every year, sea turtles lay eggs from May through August on southern beaches in the Northern Hemisphere, including the southern United States. Three types of nesting sea turtles frequent Florida waters: the green, the leatherback and the loggerhead. The loggerhead has the most nesting sites, followed by the green, then the leatherback. For example in 1999, the 5.5 miles of beach from Juno Beach, Florida to Jupiter, Florida had 5,073 loggerhead nests, 77 green turtle nests and 44 leatherback nests.

Turtles do not nest every year, so sightings and counts vary from year to year. Loggerhead turtles lay eggs two to eight times during their nesting season, with each nest having approximately 100 eggs the size and shape of ping pong balls. Turtles nest about every three years, so the loggerheads that nested this year will not come back to the beach for about three years.

Female turtles cannot lay eggs until they mature, at 20-30 years of life. Until then, all their time is spent in the water. After hatching, male turtles never come out of the water again on their own.

The female turtle crawls from the ocean at night to lay her eggs, making what is referred to as an entrance crawlway. Once above the high tide area of the beach, she digs a hole called a body pit that slopes backwards, until she hits damp sand. She then digs a deeper egg chamber with her rear flippers, and lays her eggs inside it. Most turtles face away from the water while nesting.

After her eggs are laid, she covers them with sand and tamps the sand down. She also throws sand over the body pit to cover it. In this way, she camouflages the area of the egg chamber from predators. She then turns around to go back to the ocean.

At night, from fifty-three to sixty days later, depending on the warmth of the sand, the eggs hatch and all the baby hatchlings start to dig their way out of the nest. The surface of the nest begins to heave and roll. Suddenly, a small head appears – then another and another. The whole nest becomes covered with hatchlings.

The hatchlings are attracted to light reflected off the ocean from the moon and stars, and they scurry toward it. However, artificial, man-made lights can confuse the hatchlings and lead them away from the ocean, with deadly consequences.

Even when they are not distracted from the ocean, hatchlings have a daunting task ahead of them. Beach predators such as ghost crabs and raccoons make meals of every one they catch. The hatchlings that do make it to the water face fish that cruise the shallows in search of food.

Hatchlings swim fast for the weed line, and hide in the seaweed. Once in the relative safety of the seaweed, they have to survive until they are large enough to be free from most predators.

In the years that pass from hatchling to maturity, sea turtles have been seen in various places, from the Sargasso Sea to the brackish water of the southern Intracoastal Waterway.

Most federal governments in lands where sea turtles make their nests have passed laws to protect and regulate the hunting of sea turtles and the harvesting of their nests. Even though the nests are protected, they are subject to adverse weather, natural predators and the over-development of beach areas.

Many organizations throughout the world, like The Marinelife Center of Juno Beach, are trying to help sea turtles with donations from concerned individuals. Education and research centers track the turtles' nesting habits and other key information. They teach us what we can do to help sea turtles where we live. Rehabilitation centers aid in the recovery of injured sea turtles and return them to their habitat. We can all play a part in helping these marvelous creatures survive by educating ourselves to their plight, and promoting habitat conservation.

About the Illustrator

Wildlife artist and illustrator Robin Lee Makowski grew up in the suburbs outside of Chicago, where she was exposed to a variety of wildlife. The bottlenose dolphins at Brookfield Zoo near Chicago fascinated her and sparked a life-long interest in marine mammals. Many of her illustrations have appeared in books, magazines and journals such as the Cousteau Society's *Dolphin Log, National Geographic Magazine, The New York Times,* and educational materials published by the Wild Dolphin Project and the American Cetacean Society.

Robin lived in Los Angeles, California for sixteen years, where she met her husband Mark and they raised their boys, Vincent and Matthew. Her family frequently traveled to Baja California, Mexico to camp and observe the wildlife, including the Pacific gray whales. Moving to Hobe Sound, Florida in 1992 has given Robin another perspective on local wildlife, and problems related to pollution and habitat loss.

Robin considers her talents a gift to be shared, and takes responsibility in educating the next generation in the care of our fellow creatures and the Earth we all must share.

About the Author

John Harms II was born in Dearborn, Michigan, and grew up in Palm Beach County, Florida. Many of his stories originate from his experiences as a young boy. During his youth, he spent time in the local forests and enjoyed the animals. Manatees and sea grasses were plentiful in the waterways by his home, and deserted coconut plantations gave him a colorful backdrop for his stories.

Mr. Harms II graduated from University College at the University of Florida in 1971. He went on to design and patent filtration equipment to purify water and other liquids, while compiling his adventures.

His stories educate and encourage people, especially children, to care about their environment. He visits schools often, giving presentations about writing, publishing and ecology.

His life is shared with his wife, three children, two dogs, a bird and countless fish.

Also Read Buster's Other Adventures:

Book One

The Saving of Arma Armadillo

ISBN 1-931329-00-1 (Library Bound)
ISBN 0-9653871-1-9 (Hardcover)
ISBN 0-9653871-2-7 (Softcover)

Book Two

The Saving of Valiant Blue Heron

ISBN 1-931329-01-X (Library Bound)
ISBN 0-9653871-7-8 (Hardcover)
ISBN 0-9653871-8-6 (Softcover)

Book Three

The Saving of Sly Manatee

ISBN 1-931329-02-8 (Library Bound)
ISBN 0-9653871-3-5 (Hardcover)
ISBN 0-9653871-9-4 (Softcover)

Available through bookstores and from Frederick Press

**Frederick Press
P. O. Box 32593
Palm Beach Gardens,
Florida 33420
USA**